MacKenzie Smiles, LLC, San Francisco, CA

www.mackenziesmiles.com

Originally published as *Ruffen. på nye eventyr*
Copyright © Gyldendal Norsk Forlag AS 1998 [All rights reserved]
www.gyldendal.no
First published by Den Norske Bokkluben 1977

Original text & artwork by Tor Age Bringsvaerd and Thore Hansen

Translation © Copyright James Anderson 2009

Art production by Bernard Prinz

ISBN 9780981576121

Printed in China

10 9 8 7 6 5 4 3 2 1

Distributed in the U.S. and Canada by:
Ingram Publisher Services
One Ingram Blvd.
P.O. Box 3006
LaVergne, TN 37086
(866) 400-5351

Ruffen
The Escape to Loch Ness

Tor Age Bringsvaerd
Illustrated by Thore Hansen

Far out at sea lies a mysterious island. It can only be seen on Tuesdays and Fridays. That's why it isn't on any maps. On this island is a castle, and in this castle lives an old and eminent family of sea serpents. One of the youngest sea serpents is Ruffen.

Sea serpents live in a lot of other places, too.

Sea serpents live in India...

...and in Egypt...

...in Tahiti...

...and in Mexico.

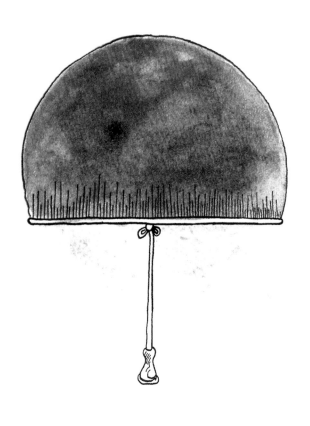

There are even sea serpents at the South Pole. But this story isn't about any of them. This story is about Ruffen and a letter he got one day.

When a sea serpent writes a letter, he puts it in an empty bottle, closes it with a cork, and throws it into the sea.

It can take a very long time to wash up in the right place, but then sea serpents are extremely patient animals. (Sometimes they get Christmas cards in the middle of the summer!)

When sea serpents need to send something quickly, they use airmail. Postman Pelican flies all over the world with his beak full of letters and packages. He always insists on postage.

For instance, it costs eight mackerel to send a letter from New York to London. With fish as stamps, Postman Pelican always has plenty to eat on his journey.

Ruffen was very excited. He'd never received an airmail letter before, and he couldn't imagine who would be writing to him.

He didn't know how to read yet, so he swam into Grandma's kitchen and asked her to help. Grandma was pretty busy. She was making fish balls with raisins. But she took the time to read the letter to him.

Loch Ness
June 6
Dear Ruffen,
I'd love you to come
visit me during
your vacation.
Hope you're well.
With much love,
Aunt Nessie
in Scotland

"I can go, can't I?" asked Ruffen.

"We'll think about it," said Grandma.

"How long will we think about it?" asked Ruffen.

"We'll see," answered Grandma.

But it didn't take long at all. That very afternoon Grandma told Ruffen he could go, and she packed him a waterproof satchel. It's a long way to Scotland.

Soon Ruffen was hitching a ride with Henry, a really big blue whale who was going Ruffen's way.

At night, Ruffen slept in the special guest room in Henry's mouth. "I enjoy a bit of company," Henry said, "so I often take passengers along. One time I had a man living here for more than three days. I think his name was Jonah. It was an awfully long time ago."

Henry had two other passengers. One was a mermaid from Spain and the other was a sea horse from China. In the evenings, they played Scrabble with Henry. Ruffen had to put Henry's letters on the board for him because a whale has no arms (and besides, they were playing inside Henry's mouth!).

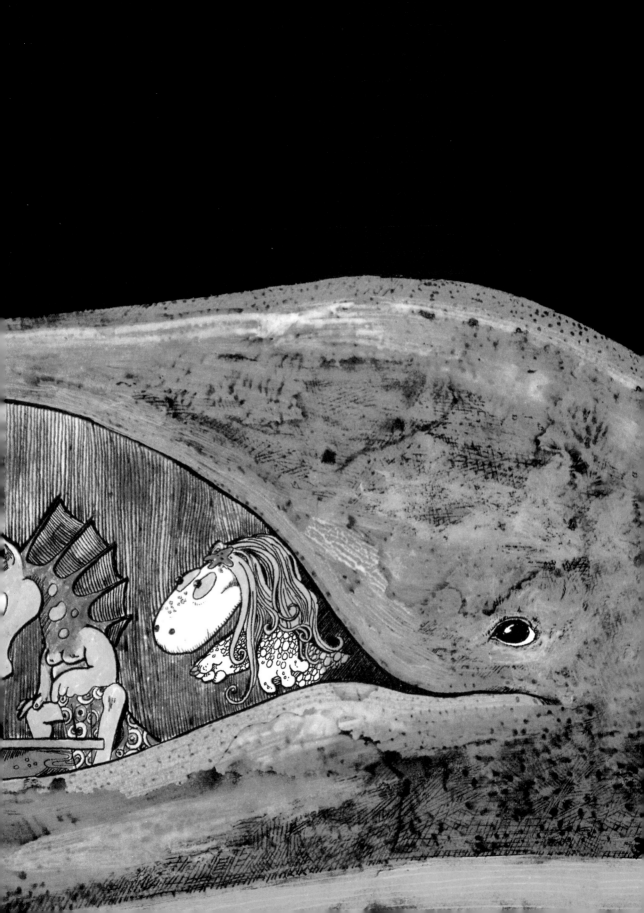

At last they arrived on the coast of Scotland and Henry dropped Ruffen off.

Ruffen still had a ways to travel. Aunt Nessie lived far from the coast in a lake called Loch Ness. (In Scotland, a lake is called a "loch".)

On dry land, sea serpents don't move very fast. A bicycle can keep up with them. Ruffen had to be very careful not to be spotted by humans. Grandma told him, "Humans are the most dangerous animals of all," although Ruffen had met a few he liked. Cautiously he made his way to Aunt Nessie's, crawling along at night and keeping himself hidden during the day.

Even so, he wasn't careful enough. One morning he woke up surrounded by humans who were pointing and shouting and screaming at him.

Ruffen tried smiling at them in a friendly way, but that just made them shout and scream even louder.

Before he knew what was happening, the humans had tied him up so tight he couldn't move or even speak.

The humans lifted him up with a crane and laid him across two trucks; he was too long for just one. Then they drove a long way to a town with such a difficult name no one even tries to say it, not even the people who live there.

The-Town-With-The-Name-No-One-Can-Say was a large zoo where Ruffen was put into a cage. Above the cage was a long sign that read:

SCALY, SCARY, SAVAGE, SELDOM-SEEN SEA SERPENT

The humans in The-Town-With-The-Name-No-One-Can-Say paid money to look at Ruffen.

Some said, "He's so scaly!"

Others said, "He's so scary!"

A few said, "He's so seldom-seen!"

They all said, "He's so scaly and scary and savage and seldom-seen!"

It wasn't long before Ruffen noticed there were a lot of other animals in the zoo, too. They were all behind great iron bars, just like he was.

"Why have the humans put us in cages?" Ruffen asked.

"The humans do whatever they want," said the elephant as he sadly shook his trunk.

"They do it just to amuse themselves," the lion snapped. "But it's no fun for us!"

"And when we get old," said the crocodile, who was crying so much he could hardly speak, "they make shoes and handbags out of us!"

"Oh, yes," sighed the elephant. "Once I had big, curvy tusks. But the humans pulled them out and made piano keys out of them!"

Ruffen listened to them all and thought, *I wonder how the humans would like it if we put them in cages! Or if we made shoes and handbags out of them! Or used their teeth for piano keys!*

When night fell upon the zoo, Ruffen pretended to be asleep, but he had a plan to escape.

As soon as the security guard had made his last rounds and everything was quiet, Ruffen got up, wrapped his tail around the strong iron bars, and pulled with all his might until he bent an opening large enough to let himself through.

Once he was out of his cage, Ruffen set free the other animals.

"What are we going to do now?" asked the rhinoceros. "The humans will surely try to recapture us and put us back in our cages."

"I have an aunt in Loch Ness," said Ruffen. "We can hide there."

"But how do we get there?" said the giraffe. "It must be a long way to Loch Ness."

"Some of us run fast, but some of us run slow," said the lion.

"And some of us can't run at all!" said the tortoise.

'Don't be frightened," said Ruffen.
'We'll just have to stick together
and help each other."

All of a sudden, Ruffen had an idea. He crawled around and emptied all the zoo's wastepaper baskets. Then he showed the other animals how to make hats by folding old newspapers.

"If we wear these hats and walk on our hind legs," Ruffen said, "people will think we're humans in funny costumes going to a fancy party!"

So they put on the hats and tiptoed out of the zoo. The bigger animals carried the ones who couldn't walk fast.

"What fantastic costumes!" people said. "They look like real animals!"

"If we had some money, we could take the bus," said the crocodile, mopping his brow. "Or a taxi." He wasn't at all used to walking so fast.

Ruffen thought for a moment. Then he had an idea. "What if we created our own transportion?" he said. "It won't be as good as a bus or a taxi, but at least it will roll!"

Ruffen lay on his tummy, stretched his neck, and raised his tail high in the air. He leaned back until his head and tail met. "See, now I'm like a wheel," said Ruffen.

The other animals looked at him in amazement.

"Get inside and hang on tight!" said Ruffen.

All together they jumped on board and off they rolled. They rolled down the street and out of The-Town-With-The-Name-No-One-Can-Say. A sea lion who had learned to read in the circus balanced on top of the wheel and read the street signs to keep them headed in the right direction.

Whenever they came to an uphill, the elephant pushed from behind.

People going to work early that morning stood by the side of the road and stared. A stranger wheel had never rolled along Scottish roads.

LOCH NESS

Suddenly Ruffen heard a car honking angrily behind him. It was the animal catchers from the zoo!

"Faster!" shouted all the animals. "Roll faster!"

"I can't," Ruffen gasped. "I'm turning as fast as I can!" The animal catchers' car came closer and closer.

The animals rolled through a small town. It was still early morning and all the houses had their curtains drawn.

As the car gained on the giant wheel, the animal catchers rubbed their hands. "We have them now!" they said to one another. "We'll catch up with them around the next corner!"

But where were the animals? Which way had they gone? The animal catchers scratched their heads. None of them thought the big sculpture in the middle of the square looked at all strange.

"They must have gone that way!" they shouted, and then drove off in the wrong direction.

When the coast was clear, the animals went rolling on their way.

Unfortunately, it wasn't long before the animal catchers were hot on the animals' heels again. By this time, the men were almost bursting with anger.

"What shall we do?" cried the animals. "Is this the end?"

Ruffen clenched his teeth and rolled as fast as he could. But the animal catchers' car got closer and closer. They had big nets and could almost reach the rolling animals.

Then the elephant had an idea. "This isn't very polite," he said shyly, "and not something we ought to do normally, but suppose all of us... you know...sort of let out a fart. I mean, there must be lots of us who need to, and it's all for a good cause." The other animals understood at once what he meant.

"One, two, three," counted the elephant. "All together now!"

And they did!

There was a rumble like the sound of fifteen motorcycles, and the smell was so awful that the animal catchers clutched their noses and fainted.

That was the last Ruffen and his friends saw of the animal catchers.

Finally the animals could relax and Ruffen had time to slow down. Some cows grazing by the side of the road invited them all for lunch.

At two-thirty that afternoon, they arrived on the shore of Loch Ness. Ruffen was so happy to see water again, being a sea serpent and all. He looked down into the water and called out, "Aunt Nessie! Are you home?"

A great head emerged from the water.

"Yes, I most certainly am," said Aunt Nessie. "Oh, how I've been worried about you. I was expecting you days ago!"

"I'll tell you the whole story later," said Ruffen. "But first, meet my new friends. Is it all right if they stay, too?"

"My goodness, yes," said Aunt Nessie. "Here in Loch Ness there's plenty of room for everyone! Come on in!"

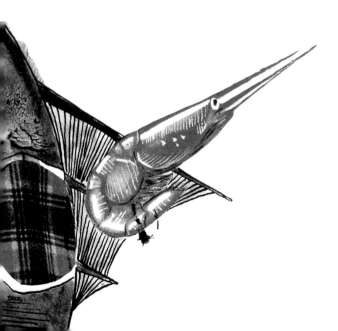

The elephant, the rhinoceros, the lion, the bear, and all the animals jumped into the loch. They held their breaths and swam under the water in a long line down to Aunt Nessie's cave.

The walls of Aunt Nessie's cave were covered in reeds, and a big chandelier made of fish bones hung from the ceiling. Aunt Nessie gave everyone eggnog and fresh-baked cookies made with kelp flour. Then she put on her best dress and her lifeboat earrings.

"You can all stay here for as long as you like," said Aunt Nessie. "We animals need to stick together. Yes, indeed, we must."

"Thank you. But we need to figure out how to get back to Africa," said the elephant.

"We'll talk about that tomorrow," said Aunt Nessie. "Tonight let's just enjoy ourselves."

And then she got out the strangest-
looking musical instrument any of
them had ever seen. She called it a
bagpipe. When she first blew into it,
it sounded like an orchestra that
had gotten lost in the forest and
couldn't find its way out. But
gradually, as Ruffen got used to the
music, he started to think it sounded
almost nice.

Aunt Nessie played on and on. She even played
some ancient Scottish tunes from the days when
she'd been young and strong and had fourteen
suitors. As she played, the other animals danced
and tapped out the rhythm.

Ruffen began to feel sleepy. He rested his head on his chest and fell asleep right where he sat. He had such a strange dream. He dreamt that Henry the whale came for a visit.

"I hear you had problems with the humans," Henry said. "Do your friends need a ride?"

Then Henry opened his mouth and the lion, the elephant, and all the other animals got in. Henry swam away, taking them on a long journey to Africa. Ruffen sat smiling as he slept because it was a good dream.

Meanwhile, Aunt Nessie blew her bagpipes all through the night until the new day dawned.

Nessie's Song

Music and English lyrics by Bob Lindstrom